Dear
Rye Library,

Thank you for putting
so much positivity
into our community!

~Susan Ross

FOR EVERY CHILD WHO IS CREATING POSITIVITY IN THE WORLD, BIG OR SMALL, THIS BOOK IS FOR YOU. YOU MAKE THE WORLD A BETTER PLACE!

This book would not have happened without my 11-year-old son, James, who tries super-hard things and bounces back from every fall with positivity and perseverance in a way that blows my mind and swells my heart. He and his brothers, Charlie (9) and George (6), have helped me to write this very special book, just for you. I couldn't be prouder of them.

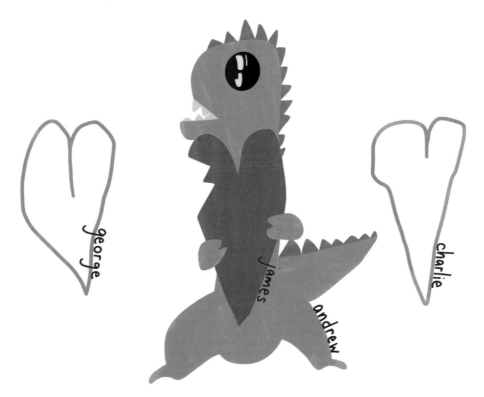

This book is dedicated to Eileen Buraczewski and the late Donna Ross, our amazing mothers who, in their own distinct ways, always chose to find the positive in life.

www.mascotbooks.com

WELCOME TO PLANET POSITIVE

For more information, please contact:
Mascot Books
620 Herndon Parkway, Suite 320
Herndon, VA 20170
info@mascotbooks.com

Library of Congress Control Number: 2021906065

CPSIA Code: PRT1121A
ISBN-13: 978-1-7368196-0-9

Printed in the United States

WELCOME TO
PLANET
POSITIVE

Written by
Susan Ross

Illustrated by
Jessica Pavelock

Have you ever noticed that you have a voice in your head that is always talking to you?
What does **YOUR** inner voice say?

"I aced my math test!"

"I helped my little sister tie her shoes."

"Wow, I scored a great goal at practice today!"

Or sometimes, "Boy, I'm hungry!"

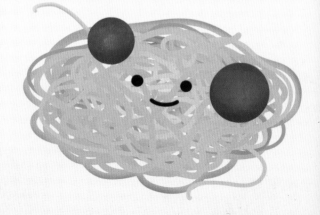

When we hear that voice,
we feel as happy as a hummingbird,
as tall as the Eiffel Tower,
and as confident as a cat.

are cats confident?

And then sometimes,
that inner voice changes into something more like,

a big hairy monster,

or a giant
Grumpity-grump.

"I could never do that,"
"I'm not good enough!"

Or, the worst—"Everyone
will laugh at me!"

Wow! That's a pretty mean monster
who would say something like that!

When we hear **THAT** voice,
we feel as embarrassed as a chicken without feathers,
as sideways as the Leaning Tower of Pisa,
and as scared as a cat.

are cats scared?

The funny thing is, that voice is just **YOU!**

It isn't good, and it isn't bad.
Who knows what's **GOOD** or **BAD?**

Your inner voice is just a reflection of how you
are **FEELING** in the moment.

But guess what?!

There's a super-special secret about feelings.

Feelings are E-motions, or Energy-in-Motion!

Ipso facto—feelings are energy!

Energy moves and changes, just like the wind.

Energy is space.

Energy is powerful.

And so are **YOU!**

did you know atoms are 99.9999% energy and only 0.0001% matter?

So, what kind of feelings and energy
do **YOU** want to have?

The answer might put a smile on your face.
Are you ready?

THE THOUGHTS YOU CHOOSE
CAN MAGICALLY FLY YOU
TO A HAPPIER PLACE...

...LIKE...!

PLANET POSITIVE!

On Planet Positive, there are lots of positive people,

like Mr. Awesome-Socks,

and lots of beautiful flowers

that grow like crazy...

...it can be messy *like spaghetti*

and feel wild and fun too!

Or would you rather go to...

PLANET POOPITY!

On Planet Poopity, everyone is super-duper negative,

like Mr. Grouchy-Pants,

and things get "stuck in the mud"

and never grow...

...it can be boring *like a rock*

and feels like everything STINKS!

If you'd like to hang out on Planet Positive,

APPLAUSE!

I have a top-notch, superhero secret for you:

S-I-M-P-L-Y choose your happy hummingbird voice!

You know, the one that makes you feel as tall as the

Eiffel Tower.

Here's a Jedi mind trick to help you find your happy hummingbird.
If you want a good voice in your head, ask yourself a really good question:

- What can I say to myself to feel awesome right now?

- What can I say to make someone smile today?

- What's one new thing I can try tomorrow?

I'd like to exchange this voice. Please send it back for a more positive one!

VOICE exchange

If a grumpy voice **STILL** pops up, follow these steps...

FIRST! Notice that grumpy voice.

And give it something special—
A SMILE!

Smile at that Grumpity-grump, and
don't stop there.

Give it a funny name!

Is it Messy Max, Negative Nancy, or Sore-loser Sam?
What about Pretend-to-be-perfect Patty?
TRY IT!

You're so silly.
Nobody's perfect!

AND VOILA! The monster voice loses its power
and starts to disappear!
Adios! Au Revoir! Sayonara! Bon Voyage!

AND THEN! Take a very big deep breath.
Not just a little breath, but an enormous breath
as big as a volcano ...like this:

Breathe in one-two-three,

hold one-two-three,

let it out one-two-three,

rest one-two-three.

AND NOW!
Your head should be as
clear as the blue sky.

If your head is
not as clear as the blue sky, do the
volcano breath thing again until you
feel as cool as a cucumber.

AND FINALLY!
For the grand finale,
what is a positive, happy hummingbird voice that you
want to hear today?

If you **STILL** need some help, great!
Please turn the page for help that comes right from
super-special, positive little people
who want to help **YOU!**

I'm an awesome kid.

Charlie's favorite

All of my problems have solutions.

James' favorite

I'm doing my BEST. Some days my BEST is bigger and taller than other days...

...And that's ok.

My mistakes help me learn and grow.

I'm super-brave for trying this hard thing.

Just go with the flow.

George's favorite

I am unstoppable!

Owen's favorite—
a favorite friend

Did you choose **YOUR** favorite positive voice? Well then...

Positive thoughts give us the gift of
happier feelings and kinder actions.

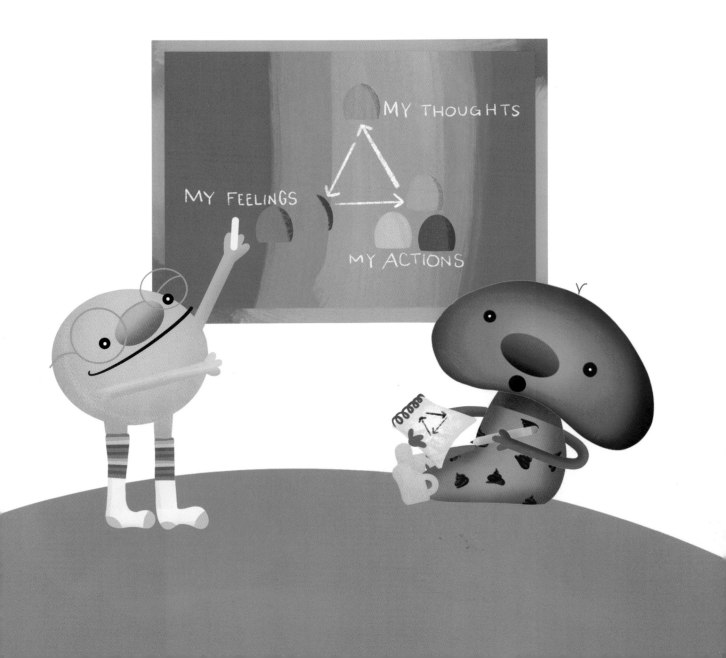

The more we hang out here together, the more we will change our world for the better. Let's lock it in with a

POSITIVE PLANET DANCE PARTY!!!

Planet Positive needs **YOU!**
And, tell your friends...
EVERYONE is **ALWAYS** welcome on Planet Positive!

THE END

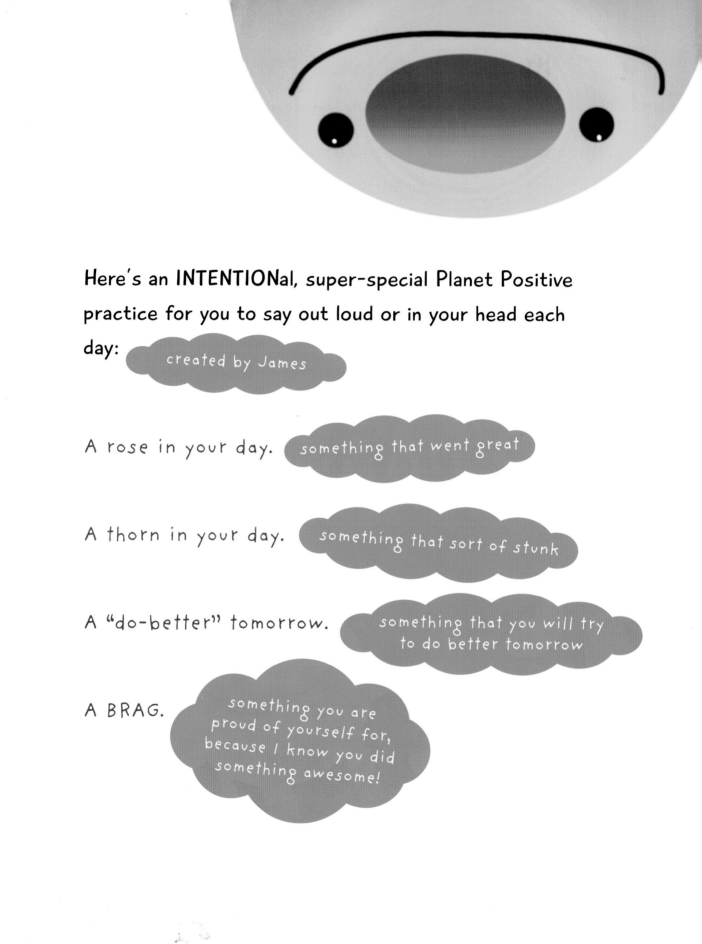

Here's an INTENTIONal, super-special Planet Positive practice for you to say out loud or in your head each day: *created by James*

A rose in your day. *something that went great*

A thorn in your day. *something that sort of stunk*

A "do-better" tomorrow. *something that you will try to do better tomorrow*

A BRAG. *something you are proud of yourself for, because I know you did something awesome!*

A NOTE OF INSPIRATION TO PARENTS

This book has been a true labor of love. It grew out of two things. First, I was inspired by a science-based coaching method I use in my work, Positive Intelligence, which is all about "mental fitness," or the capacity to respond to life's challenges with a positive mindset. In this way, everything that happens can be turned into a gift or an opportunity.

Second, and perhaps most important, I was inspired by my son who set his sights very high, tried something really hard, and, in the end, fell short and was incredibly sad and disappointed. With the help of an insightful allegory (i.e., the Stallion Story, also known as the Taoist Farmer Story—Google it!), he quickly internalized that it is up to us to decide whether something is good or bad—and accepted that what he had first seen as a failure was, in fact, an opportunity. His openness and resilience reminded me that sometimes kids can practice a positive mindset more easily than their grown-ups. They just need our support and encouragement to know that they can choose their own thoughts.

This book is an attempt to honor our children and spark the beautiful inner wisdom and creativity that lives inside each and every one of them. As they learn to dance with life's challenges, there's a lot we can teach them and a lot we can learn from them. And mostly, we can all choose to live on Planet Positive!

ABOUT THE AUTHOR & HER FAMILY

Susan Ross is a life and leadership coach and a very busy mom to three boys, James (11), Charlie (9), and George (6). She and her husband, Jeffrey Ross, are also parents to two new puppies, Buster and Bingo. They all live near the beach in Rye, New York, and they like to spend a lot of time with family and friends, often in Vermont—boating in the summer and skiing in the winter. Through it all, her family always tries their best to live on Planet Positive! Learn more about Susan at www.intentiongroup.com.

ABOUT THE ILLUSTRATOR

Jessica Pavelock is an illustrator focusing on animal and nature themes. She fell in love with picture book art during her years as a pre-K teacher and is thrilled to now be creating her own illustrations. When she isn't creating, she loves hiking, observing wildlife, taking photos, and seeking out vegan restaurants. She lives in New York City with her husband, Alex, and two mischievous cats, Shane and Jefferson. View more of Jessica's work at www.zyracat.com.